2003

W9-BYA-799

The Princesses Have a Ball

WRITTEN BY Teresa Bateman

ILLUSTRATED BY Lynne Cravath

Albert Whitman and Company
Morton Grove, Illinois

Library of Congress Cataloging-in-Publication Data

Bateman, Teresa.

The princesses have a ball / by Teresa Bateman ; illustrated by Lynne Cravath.

p. cm.

Summary:

In this rhyming update of the fairy tale of the "Twelve Dancing Princesses,"

twelve princesses wear out their shoes playing basketball.

ISBN 0-8075-6626-8

[1. Fairy tales. 2. Princesses — Fiction. 3. Basketball — Fiction.]

I. Twelve dancing princesses English. II. Cravath, Lynne Woodcock, ill. III. Title.

PZ8.B3015 Pr 2002   [398.2—dc21]   2002000777

Published in 2002 by Albert Whitman & Company,

6340 Oakton Street, Morton Grove, Illinois 60053-2723.

Published simultaneously in Canada by General Publishing, Limited, Toronto.

Printed in the United States of America.

10 9 8 7 6 5 4 3 2 1

The text font is Fontesque Bold.

The design is by Scott Piehl.

For more information about Albert Whitman and Company,

visit our web site at www.albertwhitman.com.

But they didn't dance,
as a point of pride,
and their dainty step
was a healthy stride.

Then one morning when
the girls took their place,
every princess shoe
was a pure disgrace.
With the satin ripped,
and the ribbons torn,
and the instep stripped,
and the sole all worn.

Once upon a time,
not so long ago,
there were twelve sweet princesses
all in a row.
Though their dad was short
they were growing tall,
and the king remarked,
"This won't do at all!
Why, to catch a prince
you should be petite,
dance and walk with grace,
and have tiny feet."

To Alyssa, Cassie, Jennifer, Jody, Shelley, Rachel, Katherine, and Jessica—
who all know how to wear out their shoes, having a ball!

— T. B.

To my two favorite princesses, Chlöe and Carrie.

— L. C.

"What goes on at night?
What do you girls do,
that would wear a hole
into every shoe?
You should be asleep,"
fussed the king, "I say—
dreaming of a prince,
and your wedding day."

Princesses should not
have their toes in view.
So new shoes were bought—
they were ruined, too!
For the next three weeks
it went on that way,
with their shoes worn out
each and every day.

"Now I've had enough,"
said their dad, "I fear
there is something strange
going on 'round here."

So the puzzled king
sent out a decree
asking for a key
to this mystery.

Soon the halls were filled
with detectives whose
only mission was
to explain those shoes.

One believed disguise
would reveal the truth,
but the girls caught on
and threw out that sleuth!

And another hoped
he could track them down,
but the girls made friends
with his well-trained hound.

There were spies, and traps—
but no clever plot
could outwit those girls.
They would not be caught!

Now a man named Jack,
of the cobbler trade,
saw the ragged shoes
that the king displayed.
Jack remarked, "It's strange,
but it's clear to me
that these shoes were worn out
athletically."

Jack just had to know
how the deed was done,
so he crept past guards
as the clock struck one.
In the princesses' room
he was not surprised
to see empty beds
that had been disguised.
Through the closet door,
standing open wide,
lay a passageway,
so Jack went inside.

Then a *thump-thump-thump*
shook the passage walls,
and he tiptoed up
and saw

In a basement room,
as the night grew short,
were a dozen girls
on a makeshift court.
They made up two teams,
with two substitutes.
And they ran and passed
and they shouted, "SHOOT!"

When the game was done
and the girls were through,
there was not a sole
left on any shoe.
Jack slipped silently
out the way he came—
for he knew a way
to improve their game.

He designed a shoe
with a rubber sole,
and a high-topped edge
to stop ankle roll.
He put arch supports
in the proper places,
and ditched pink ribbons
for sturdy laces.

When the order came
for new princess shoes,
Jack packed up the ones that
he hoped they'd choose.
When he placed the shoes
on the palace floor,
all the girls went, "OOH!
Could you make us more?"

Then the youngest said,
with her eyes aglow,
"How did you find out?
Tell me, how'd you know?"
"I can hold my tongue,"
Jack replied. "But, hey!
Why not tell your dad?
He should see you play!"

She looked glum. "I doubt
he'd give us a chance
when he thinks a 'ball'
is a kind of dance!"
Jack just smiled and said,
"All you girls are strong,
don't you think it's time
that you proved him wrong?"
Then she grinned. "Hey girls!
Let's put on a show!"
When they heard her plan,
they were all gung ho!

So they asked the king,
on his royal throne,
"Can we plan a ball
of our very own?"

Then they locked the door
to the ballroom tight,
and they worked inside
morning, noon, and night.

When the day arrived
for their special ball,
guests were quite surprised
when they saw the hall.

As they took their seats
in their fancy dress,
they looked all around
for their hostesses.

Then a bell rang out,
and in shirts and shorts,
princesses appeared
up and down the court.

They were crisp and clean
as they showed their skills,
dribbling up and down,
running passing drills.

And they played a game
that the crowd adored
as they spun and passed,
and they shot and scored.

All the people's cheers
filled the castle hall.
"This is something new!
It's a *basket*-ball!"

Then the king stepped down
from his royal throne,
and he said, "My girls,
I wish I had known.
Even royalty is allowed some fun,
and I'm proud of you,
each and every one."

Now their life is just
as the girls would choose.
They all play the game—
Jack designs their shoes.
Since the referee
also needs a pair,
there are special shoes
for the king to wear.

And the princesses
get their sleep at night—
playing games by day
to their hearts' delight.

THE END